Hey, Zeke- you missin' any teeth?

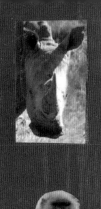

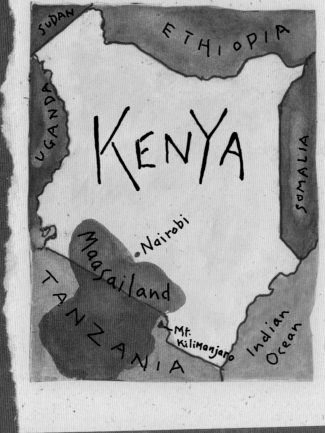

KeNYa

SUDAN

ETHIOPIA

UGANDA

SOMALIA

Nairobi

Maasailand

TANZANIA

Mt. Kilimanjaro

Indian Ocean

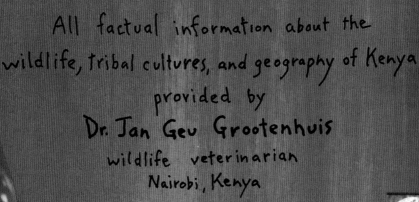

All factual information about the
wildlife, tribal cultures, and geography of Kenya
provided by
Dr. Jan Geu Grootenhuis
wildlife veterinarian
Nairobi, Kenya

SAFARI
JOURNAL

The Adventures in Africa
of
Carey Monroe

by
Hudson Talbott

Silver Whistle
Harcourt, Inc.
New York

San Diego   London

my first "souvenir"—

African Game Checklist

Today I saw

Animal	Swahili Name	
Elephant	Ndovu	☐
Lion	Simba	☐
Rhino	Kifaru	☐
Buffalo	Nyati	☐
Leopard	Chui	☐
Cheetah	Duma	☐
Hippo	Kiboko	☐
Giraffe	Twiga	☐
Zebra	Punda Mlia	☐
Thomson's gazelle	Swara Tomi	☐
Impala	Swara Pala	☐
Eland	Pofu	☐
Hartebeest	Kongoni	☐
Wildebeest	Nyumbu	☐
Baboon	Nyani	☐
Colobus	Mbega	☐
Hyena	Fisi	☐
Crocodile	Mamba	☐
Warthog	Ngiri	☐
Ostrich	Mbuni	☐
Flamingo	Flamingo	☐

—got it from a tour leader passing them out on the plane —she thought I was with her group!

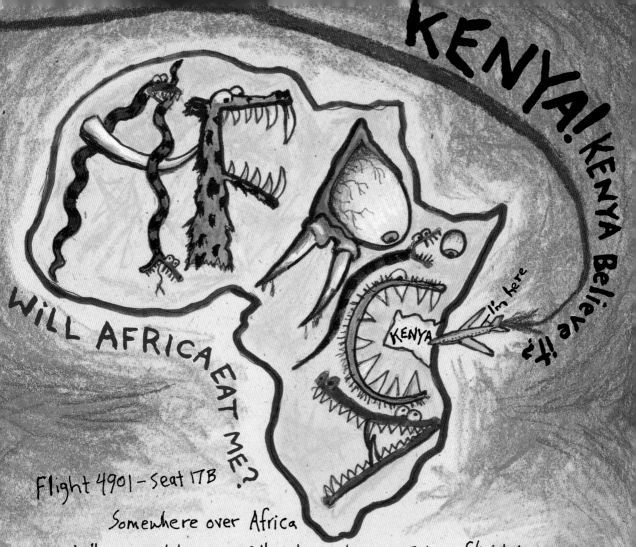

KENYA! KENYA Believe it?

WILL AFRICA EAT ME?

I'm here

KENYA

Flight 4901 - Seat 17B

Somewhere over Africa

What am I doing here? How long does a 17-hour flight take when you're sitting next to a guy who smells like he died 3 days ago? What did I say that sounded like "I want to go to Africa with Aunt Elaine?" Uh-oh, here she comes again, down the aisle, jangling her 300 bracelets. Wait till she gets a whiff of stinky Dr. Fatso, next to me here! So, why, you may ask, am I going to Africa with my aunt? "Because animal prints are big this year." That's the way she talks. She used to be a model — now she just photographs them, in really strange places. Dad calls her a "fashionista." She is **not** normal. She calls me her anniversary present to Mom & Dad, meaning they're getting a Caribbean cruise without me and Sally. Sally is getting riding camp, because she gets everything she wants. And me? I'm getting a headache, thinking about 2 weeks with wacky Aunt Elaine!

It's not that she's really **nuts**. I know she likes me, at least she likes giving me stuff, like a cool new camera and this journal book. But then she goes all wacky and says things like "I can see in your AURA that you're a writer. Start your life story, daaaarling."

Yeah, right. What life? I'm 12½ years old! I get up. I go to school. I play video games. You call that a life? You think I would be here if I had one?

She did give me an idea, though. I'll need to find something to do for the next 2 weeks (anything would beat tagging along behind the fashionista crew). It might be fun to keep a notebook about the animals I see here. I could try to find every animal on that "African Game Checklist." It won't be my life story, but my **wildlife** story! Starring the BIG FIVE! The lion, the elephant, the rhino, the leopard, and the buffalo — those are the ones the tour books say you gotta see if you go on safari in Kenya. "**Safari**" is my first word in Swahili — it means "travel or journey." My second word is "kifaru" — means "rhinoceros" — I found it on the game list after hearing the fat guy next to me (the infamous Dr. Fatso) repeat it over and over on his little phoney-phone. Now he's got his laptop open — he's looking at some kind of price list. This could be interesting. I'll keep my head down and act like I'm just writing. Wow! It's a list of animal body parts! They're expensive! He's highlighted rhino horn — $5000 a pound!

We just landed! I'm actually looking out at Africa. Boy, it really is the **Dark Continent**. Maybe that's because it's 1:30 in the morning. There's supposed to be a charter plane waiting to "whisk" us to the first photo location — Amboseli National Park. It's the home to the "stars" of my new epic. I already have the title for it! Wait till Hollywood sees this!!!

I've been awake for about an hour - jet lag, I guess. But something else is starting to sink in - Africa is out there and I'm getting antsy to see it. The driver with Aunt Elaine's van won't be here till after breakfast. He's kind of a cool guy. His name is Mutongai. He was waiting for us with the van when our charter plane landed in a field here in Amboseli National Park. I liked him right away because he let me sit next to him in the front seat so I could get away from the Fabulons (that's my new word for Wack-El's "people" - they're from the Planet Fabulous and that's the only word they use there). I showed Mutongai my "Game Checklist" and he said he could tell me stuff about every animal on the list. He's also a game scout, so he knows where to find them. I think I'm gonna take a little walk and see what I find.

6:00 A.M. - Outside the lodge gates

There's a real racket all around me. I'm sitting on the bank of a creek, and there are all kinds of weird animal calls - I guess everybody's waking up. The road I followed leads to a little village on the other side of the creek. I think it's for the lodge's staff people. There's a kid over there watching me. He looks about my age. I wonder if he's ever seen a Frisbee.

Later

Well, if he had never seen a Frisbee before, he sure figured it out quick. I took mine out of my backpack and tossed it over the creek. He picked it up and threw it right back. The next time I threw it he caught it and sent it right back to me. We were tossing it back and forth until - SPLASH - it had to happen - it landed right in the middle of the creek. I started to wade in for it, but the kid went nuts! "NO! NO! MAMBA! MAMBA!"

He was yelling that at me. And I'm thinking "who's Mamba?"

WOMP

My newest Swahili word: MAMBA = crocodile!

Out of nowhere two giant jaws chomped down on my Frisbee! I jumped back so fast I fell down. The kid was bug-eyed and gasping, but so was I. We kept staring at the chewed-up Frisbee that the croc spit out, then looked at each other, and burst out laughing. But then I heard the van screech on its brakes behind me.

Busted.

"I see you've met my son," said Mutongai. He was _not_ laughing. I tried to explain that I started it, but he was already shouting at his son.

"He is with me to learn the ways of tracking the wildlife," Mutongai said. "This is not the way."

I climbed into the van and we drove to the bridge where the kid slowly climbed in next to me. We shook hands and tried not to laugh. He said his name was Pilot, because he wants to fly.

"Yes, away from his chores!" added Mutongai. He finally cracked a smile. I asked him to **PLEASE** not tell my aunt about the croc. He said he wouldn't, but only if I promise not to wander off on my own again. Deal.

Then he said we could go on a game drive because he wasn't needed till after breakfast, and this was the best time to see animals. At dawn.

Amboseli

My First Elephant!

The sun is just about to rise. We're driving slowly so we don't disturb the big "tusker" on the right. Mutongai said it's a bull. They wander alone and can be unpredictable. He flapped his ears as we drove by - Mutongai said that meant "back off." There are close to 700 elephants here at Amboseli.

Mt. Kilimanjaro

the "shining mountain"
19,340 ft. — (5,895 meters)
It's the highest mountain in
Africa, and the largest free-standing
mountain in the world. It's
actually a dormant volcano.
No matter where we drive here, "Kili"
is always in view — even though it's
many miles away in Tanzania.

Mutongai said all this land once belonged to his people - the Maasai.
The reason why there is so much wildlife here is because the
Maasai kept it open, never fencing it. They raise cattle, and move their
herds to wherever the grazing is good. That works for wildlife, too. But
only 25% of Kenya's wildlife live on protected land, like Amboseli. The rest roam
around looking for food, and can get into trouble when they wander into a farm.

ELEPHANT ~ NDOVU
(swahili)

Notes

Elephants are so quiet! We were watching some birds and didn't even notice this herd drifting out of the trees behind us until Mutongai heard some twigs snapping. He said that they communicate with each other through very low vibrations that we can't even hear, called "infrasound." They can stay in touch with each other, even if they're several miles apart. So who needs cellphones?

Mutongai said no other animals mess with elephants, not even lions. They're the real kings of the beasts-and they're led by a queen! The leader is the smartest and oldest female, called the "matriarch", and the herd members are her female relatives and their kids. Family groups usually have about 12 adults (cows) and their kids (calves) but groups can stay in touch with each other and gather together at a water hole for "happy hour"

ELEPHANT TYPES

AFRICAN
sway back
larger ears

ASIAN
humpback
small ears

AMERICAN
video game

WHITE
gift from Aunt Edna

We watched the teenage females "babysitting" their younger brothers and sisters while their mothers bathed. Two teenage males were play-fighting, chasing each other around, and annoying everyone in the herd. Mutongai said the queen will kick them out soon. Then they'll start wandering alone – in search of their first "date".

He's so not my type

here he comes!

Cattle egrets wait for insects jumping out of the grass as elephants pass by.

ELEPHANT STATS:

Size: 6ft. to 12ft. at shoulder

weight: up to 7 tons! (that's 2 SUV's)

trunk: a nose that acts like an arm, tips are "fingers", can grab twigs & grass

tusks: long teeth on males & females - used for defense

habitat: plains and woodlands, always near water

LION ~ SIMBA

NOTES

(Swahili)

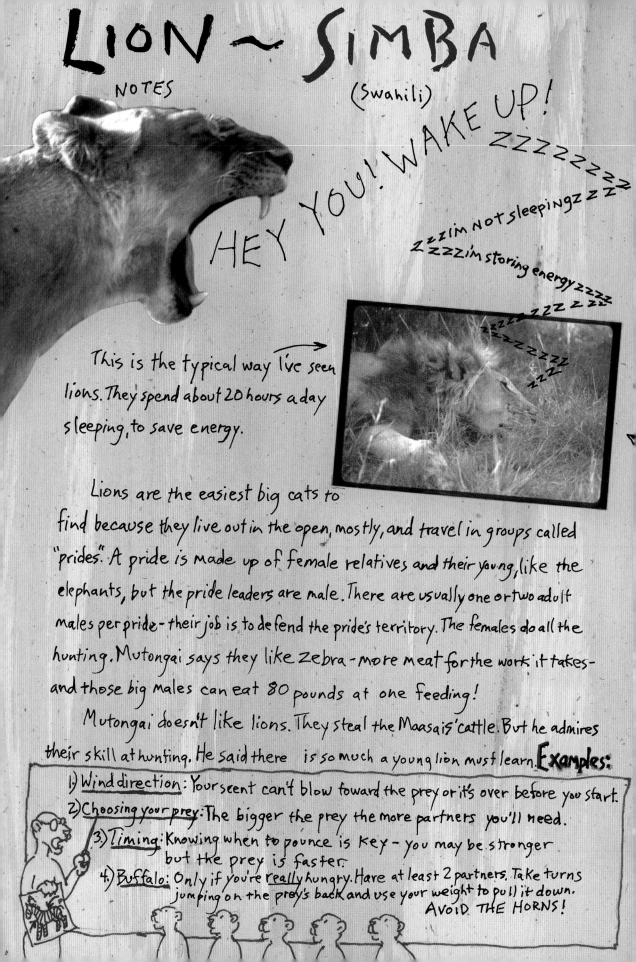

HEY YOU! WAKE UP!

ZZZZZZZZ

ZZZ Im not sleeping Z ZZ

ZZZZ Im storing energy ZZZZ

This is the typical way I've seen lions. They spend about 20 hours a day sleeping, to save energy.

Lions are the easiest big cats to find because they live out in the open, mostly, and travel in groups called "prides". A pride is made up of female relatives and their young, like the elephants, but the pride leaders are male. There are usually one or two adult males per pride - their job is to defend the pride's territory. The females do all the hunting. Mutongai says they like zebra - more meat for the work it takes - and those big males can eat 80 pounds at one feeding!

Mutongai doesn't like lions. They steal the Maasais' cattle. But he admires their skill at hunting. He said there is so much a young lion must learn. **Examples:**

1) <u>Wind direction</u>: Your scent can't blow toward the prey or it's over before you start.

2) <u>Choosing your prey</u>: The bigger the prey the more partners you'll need.

3) <u>Timing</u>: Knowing when to pounce is key - you may be stronger but the prey is faster.

4) <u>Buffalo</u>: Only if you're <u>really</u> hungry. Have at least 2 partners. Take turns jumping on the prey's back and use your weight to pull it down. AVOID THE HORNS!

The Hectic Life of the Pride Leader

posing →

← storing energy

marking territory →

Just like when Scruffy sprayed the couch! (he's fixed now)

LION ● STATS

<u>height</u>: 3 to 4 ft. at shoulder

<u>weight</u>: females – up to 250 pounds

males – up to 500 pounds

<u>length</u>: 8 ft. to 11 ft. (with tail)

<u>habitat</u>: grasslands, open woodland

<u>prides</u>: 2 to 40 animals – lions are

the only <u>cats</u> who live in social groups

<u>hunting</u>: mostly after dark - it's cooler &

their night-vision is 6 times stronger than ours

<u>roar</u>: males do it to claim territory

you can hear a lion roar 5 miles

away – ALL NIGHT LONG!

Hyenas - Lion Enemy #1

a hate-hate relationship

They wait for lions to make a kill and then try to steal it. They have the strongest jaws in Africa – 500 lbs. of pressure per sq. inch!

Thanks for lunch! What's for dinner?

Hee-hee-hee! Just remember, we're not laughing <u>with</u> you, we're laughing <u>at</u> you! HA HA HA HA!

BUFFALO ~ NYATI

    Of the Big Five, this guy seems to have the least to worry about. According to Mutongai, the African buffalo is the least endangered but perhaps the <u>most dangerous</u> of all. When this guy saw me looking at him, he pulled himself out of his watering hole and stared back at me. Mutongai told me to quickly take the picture so we could leave before he decided to charge into our car. Mutongai has seen buffalos flip lions over their backs with those nasty horns. He said there are many stories about hunters being gored by buffalos that the hunters shot and mistook for dead. Maybe they're not as dumb as they look.

Hey, punk, what you starin' at? You wanna piece o' me?

Buffalo   Stats:

Height: 3-5ft. at shoulder
Length: 8-10ft.
Weight: 450 - 1,500 lbs.
Habitat: open grasslands
Habits: They live in family groups of 12 or more and join up with large herds, numbering several thousand. Herd members will defend each other against predator attack.

Rhinoceros ~ KIFARU

side-view

Of all the animals on my list, I think the rhino has the saddest story. Because they're so big and live out in the open they've always been easy to hunt. And now there are only a few thousand left in Africa and only a few hundred in Kenya. Why? It's the horn. In one country a rhino horn dagger handle is a top status symbol, so the horn is the main target of poaching. I told Mutongai about the guy on the plane (Dr. Fatso) researching rhino horn prices. He told me to tell him if I ever see Fatso in the lodge. Hmmm.....

2 Rhino types in Africa

A. Black rhino - smaller, lives in bushland, has pointy lip for snagging twigs & leaves

B. White rhino - name comes from "wide" because it has a wide mouth, for grazing

A. B.

Rhino Stats:

Height: 3½ – 6½ ft. at the shoulder

Length: 9½ – 13½ ft.

Weight: 2,000 – 5,000 pounds

LEOPARD · CHUI
Notes   (swahili)

I actually saw **2** different
leopards today! That's really
incredible luck - they're hardly out in the
open, in the daytime. They're night hunters.
Mutongai said little is known about leopards because
they are so secretive and shy. He warned me that if I got out of
the car to take the cat's picture the cat would run away. It did. I
barely set foot on the ground and the cat was a vapor trail. I thought
they were going to be leaping out of trees at <u>me</u>, like in the
Tarzan movies. But Kenya isn't really like Tarzan movies.
It's more like <u>National Geographic</u> with smells.

↑

This guy had totally pigged out on that gazelle he had dragged up in the tree. He was so zonked that he didn't even know that I was below on the ground, taking his picture. Leopards are the best climbers of the cats. They like to drag their kills up into trees, to keep lions and hyenas from stealing them. They're so strong they can even drag away a horse. Mutongai said they're not as picky about where they live and what they eat, which probably gives them a better chance of survival. They'll take whatever they can - Maasai goats, for example. I guess that's why Mutongai doesn't like the leopard - it really gets his goat!

Leopard 🔘 Stats:

Height: 2ft. to 2ft. 4 in at shoolder
Weight: 60 to 150 pounds
Length: body: 3-4 ft., tail: about 30 in.
Habitat: deep forest to dry scrubland
Habits: solitary, except for a mom with cubs.
"Black panthers" are solid black leopards

GIRAFFE ~ TWIGA
NOTES
(in Swahili)

Giraffes are the look outs of the savanna. Mutongai said their eyesight is very good, and being so tall, they can see danger coming from far away. The other animals keep an eye on the way giraffes are acting. If they get "spooked", then everybody starts moving.

Tongues

mine: 2"

giraffe: 18"

The longest tongue of all land mammals - they can rip off small branches with it.

Neck bones

giraffe: 7

me: 7

GIRAFFE STATS:

height: 14 ft. to 19 ft.

weight: 1,750 to 2,800 pounds

habitat: grasslands, bush country

food: mostly leaves - they're so tall so they can browse on the higher limbs

speed: up to 35 m.p.h.

family groups: mothers and their kids stay together until the young males join their own groups. Adult males roam alone.

RETICULATED GIRAFFE
(rare around here, lives further north)

"Necking"
Young males bang their necks into each other, testing who's fiercer - like trading punches.

Drinking

Difficult and scary this is when lions can get them.

Babies

They're 6 ft. tall and 150 lbs. when they're born! That's as big as Mutongai!

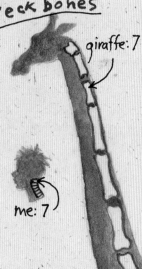

MAASAI GIRAFFES

CHEETAH ~ DUMA

NOTES (swahili)

My favorite - the coolest of the cool. It's obvious what the cheetah's specialty is - <u>SPEED</u>. They're the fastest animal on land - clocked at 70 m.p.h.!

They can't sustain that speed for long, so they have to use it wisely. They stalk their prey as far as they can and then charge full blast toward their target. They try to trip their prey by hooking a claw into the prey's leg, but the prey's trick is to run all zig-zaggy.

BUILT FOR

Non-retractable claws -

- better for fast traction!

Cheetah Stats:

Height: 2½ - 3 ft. at shoulder

Length: 3 ft. 9 in. - 5 ft. with tail

Weight: 77 - 143 pounds

Eyesight: excellent

Voice: no roar, but they growl, hiss, and "chirp" like birds to call the cubs

Families: Cubs stay with mothers for about 2 years.

Why the spots?

Here's why ↗

The spots blend into the pattern of light and shadows in the bushes and tall grass, making them hard to "spot"!

big lunch →

SPEED

If the cheetah hasn't downed the prey within 300yds. they have to quit and catch their breath. They also lose a lot of their meals to lions and hyenas. But Mutongai said the cheetah's biggest problem is loss of habitat. So much of their former range has become farms and ranches. According to Mutongai they just don't adapt as easily as lions and leopards to changes in their environment. There are only 250-300 cheetahs in the Mara-Serengeti region, compared to 3,000 lions and over 9,000 hyenas. There are only about 12,000 cheetahs left in the whole world. They could all be gone by the time I'm a grown-up. It's hard to believe such an amazing animal could disappear forever.

11:45 P.M. — the last night in Amboseli

I'm wiped out from today, but I want to write down what I
remember of a talk I had with Mutongai, while it's still fresh. I got
kinda bummed this morning, for the first time since I came.
We were watching this great pair of cheetah brothers when a
whole line of tourist buses showed up and surrounded them.

"Why can't they find their own cheetahs?" I griped.
"How can these poor guys hunt with so many people watching?"

I hated what I saw. But the other tourists were probably thinking the same thing. "I guess I'm part of the problem, too," I said.

"Problem?" Mutongai said. "You may be the cheetah's best friend
right now. They are living on borrowed time, and it's the tourists

who are lending it to them."

I guess he could tell he had lost me, because he went on.

"The world keeps changing, and only those who can change with it survive. Change doesn't have to be a bad thing, but, for some of us, it is not so easy..."

"Do you mean the cheetah?" I asked, "...or the Maasai?"

"The world has come to our door, too," he said. "It is up to us to find a place for ourselves in it, if we are to survive."

"Maybe we come because you have something we don't have," I said, "like a cheetah."

He nodded and said, "That is my point. Everyone wants to see the great animals roaming freely, but that's not the way the world is anymore. Except in a few places. The Maasailand is still open. Visitors would see how abundant the wildlife still is there, and how we live with it peacefully."

"But you told me the Maasai warriors killed lions," I said. "You call that peaceful?"

"When a lion steals a Maasai cow it is very hard for us, but we are trying to look at the bigger picture," he said. "The tribal councils pay for cows lost to lions. Some of our precious grazing lands have become wildlife conservation areas where all animals can live, protected by Maasai. One community has even imported two rhinos, which are nearly extinct in the wild. Those rhinos mean hope to us. If we can attract visitors to our lands perhaps we will claim a place for ourselves in the modern world, and perhaps for the cheetahs, too."

Video cameras give me such indigestion!

Ptooooooi

There was more to that talk but that's the part that stuck with me. It made me wonder what "the modern world" would look like to them— through Maasai eyes. What do they see? What could it mean to be a member of a tribe in the 21st century?

I don't think being Presbyterian counts.

Tomorrow we fly back to Nairobi for the weekend, and then catch another charter plane to the next stop—

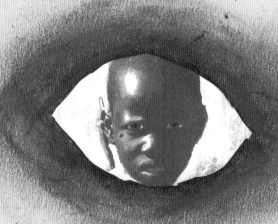

the Maasai Mara Reserve. Mutongai and Pilot will be going overland in the equipment van and we'll meet up with them next week. For me it means having to deal with the Fabulons for a whole weekend on my own. So far I've only run into them at break- fast and dinner with Aunt Elaine. I spend every day with Pilot and his dad "game scouting". They've really saved me. We talk about everything. I can tell Pilot doesn't really get why I want to take pictures of animals and stick them in this book but it gives him a chance to play with my Game Boy. He cracks me up. I wish I could just hang with them for the rest of the trip. There may be a way – but I can't think now. My eyes have become slits. More tomorrow in Nairobi or...

<u>Sat. A.M.</u> – **FREE!** I did it!!!

Good ol' wacky Aunt Elaine – so caring, so scattered. I knew if I just hung back and let the Fabs do their thing all would go well – it did. When the van came to pick everybody up there was enough chaos going on to lose an elephant.

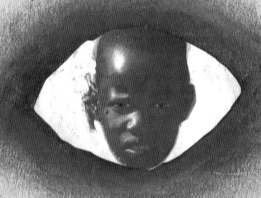

All I had to do was to "go invisible." Out of sight, out of mind. And "out of mind" is where Aunt Elaine lives. She was on the plane before she even noticed I was missing. She called Mutongai in a panic, but he calmed her right down and told her I had found him after I had "missed" the van. Then he said he could:

A) put me on another plane, which would mean losing a day

B) drive me to Nairobi himself, which would also mean losing a day

C) take me with them on the overland trip to the Maasai Mara!

Bless that wacky aunt! She went for **C**! We leave in an hour! I'm going on safari with Maasais in Maasailand!!!

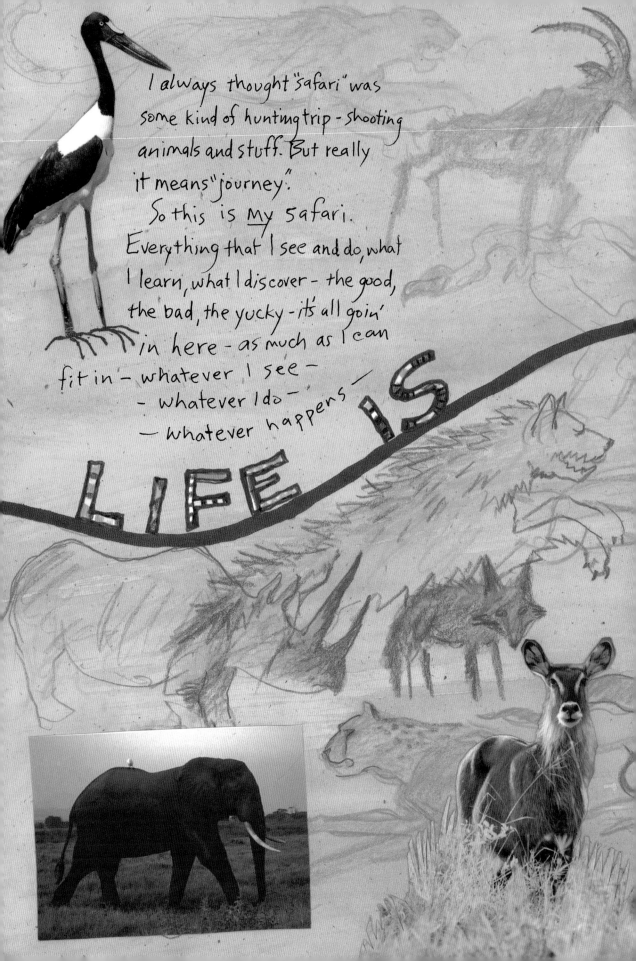

I always thought "safari" was
some kind of hunting trip - shooting
animals and stuff. But really
it means "journey".
So this is My safari.
Everything that I see and do, what
I learn, what I discover - the good,
the bad, the yucky - it's all goin'
in here - as much as I can
fit in - whatever I see -
— whatever I do —
— whatever happens —

LIFE IS

A SAFARI

We're heading into the heart of Maasailand. Mutongai keeps telling me I "haven't seen anything yet." As great as Amboseli is, it's nothing compared to where we're going — the Maasai Mara. But after all, it is his home-land. We'll be crossing the Rift Valley — the Continental Divide of Africa — like the Rockies, except it goes down instead of up.

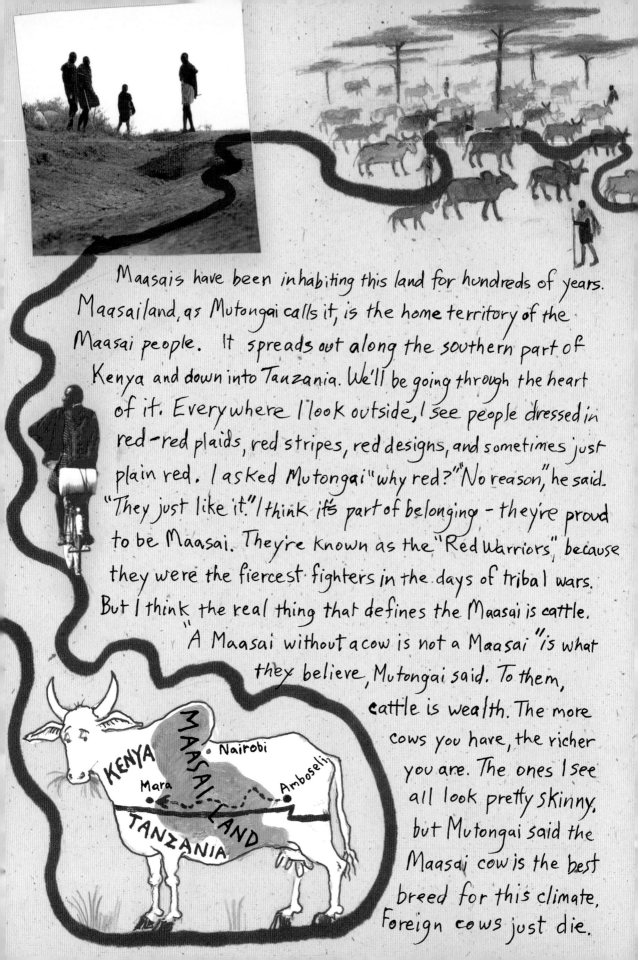

Maasais have been inhabiting this land for hundreds of years. Maasailand, as Mutongai calls it, is the home territory of the Maasai people. It spreads out along the southern part of Kenya and down into Tanzania. We'll be going through the heart of it. Everywhere I look outside, I see people dressed in red - red plaids, red stripes, red designs, and sometimes just plain red. I asked Mutongai "why red?" "No reason," he said. "They just like it." I think it's part of belonging - they're proud to be Maasai. They're known as the "Red Warriors", because they were the fiercest fighters in the days of tribal wars. But I think the real thing that defines the Maasai is cattle.

"A Maasai without a cow is not a Maasai" is what they believe, Mutongai said. To them, cattle is wealth. The more cows you have, the richer you are. The ones I see all look pretty skinny, but Mutongai said the Maasai cow is the best breed for this climate. Foreign cows just die.

KENYA
MAASAILAND
TANZANIA
Nairobi
Mara
Amboseli

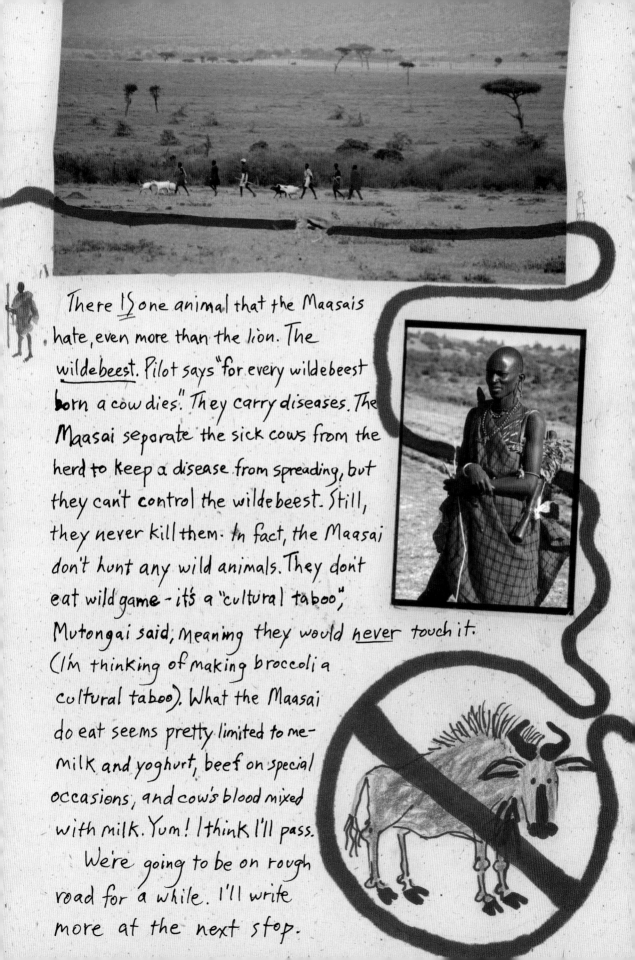

There IS one animal that the Maasais hate, even more than the lion. The wildebeest. Pilot says "for every wildebeest born a cow dies." They carry diseases. The Maasai separate the sick cows from the herd to keep a disease from spreading, but they can't control the wildebeest. Still, they never kill them. In fact, the Maasai don't hunt any wild animals. They don't eat wild game - it's a "cultural taboo," Mutongai said, meaning they would never touch it. (I'm thinking of making broccoli a cultural taboo). What the Maasai do eat seems pretty limited to me - milk and yoghurt, beef on special occasions, and cow's blood mixed with milk. Yum! I think I'll pass.

We're going to be on rough road for a while. I'll write more at the next stop.

2:30 P.M. - the Mutongai family "Manyatta"

At last! A chance to stretch my legs after 4 hours on the road (if you can call it a road - we left pavement about 2 hours ago). We're now at the manyatta of Pilot's grandfather. The family is inside visiting, so it gives me a chance to write and take pictures. Mutongai said to always ask before pointing the camera at the grown-ups, so I'll draw them - it's easier.

A manyatta is a "family village". I think that everybody living here is related - uncles, great-uncles, cousins, aunts, cousins,

Pilot's cousin →

half brothers, cousins, step-grandmothers, cousins, cousins, and cousins. They like big families here. Mutongai said when he was my age that families with 16 kids was normal. Now, it's more like 5 or 6. It was also normal for the men to have many wives! Mutongai said he just has one and he plans to keep it that way. I imagine Mrs. Mutongai plans the same thing.

The Maasai women are great homemakers - literally! They're <u>home</u> <u>makers</u>. Besides milking the cows, gathering wood, cooking, and cleaning, the women build the houses, using sticks and branches woven together, and then plastering over the woven wood with mud and cow dung. For the Maasai and their cows there's no such thing as "waste"!

THE MANYATTA

women using the fence for a clothes line

Kids watch the goats

goats

Pilot's house

Cows come inside at night

house

house

house

house

store house

man counting cows

woman carrying huge load of wood

This is what the manyatta would look like from overhead. The fence circling the houses is made of very thorny branches, stacked up over six feet high. It keeps the cows in and the lions out. Well, that's the idea, anyway. The herds leave in the morning to graze in the open pasture land and come back inside before nightfall. The men and older boys go with the cattle. The younger kids go with the goats and sheep. The Maasai are "semi-nomadic," meaning they stay in one place while the grazing is good then move on, to greener pastures.

a tiny window for the smoke

Girls' bed

Boys' bed

door

calves and lambs come inside at night

Pilot's House

Maasai houses are all about the same size – "cozy." The mother and girls have a bed on one side and the Dad and boys are on the other. The cooking is done over an open fire, right in the middle of the floor. The smoke goes out a tiny window - the only window. There's a stall for the calves, lambs, and kid goats. They're brought inside at night for warmth and safety.

Pilot just came running with news there's a big event going on at a nearby manyatta. He said that EVERYBODY is over there right now, including the big "laibon".
Wow! Cool!

What's a laibon?

The LAIBON

The laibon is the wise man of the Maasai.
They say he can tell the future.

He's 99 yrs. old!

the white
triangles protect
his thoughts from
his enemies

the lion's tail
whisk is a
symbol of his
authority

the gourd holds
"magic" stones
which he tosses
to read the future

Mutongai said that besides giving advice, the laibon's most
important job is setting up the different levels or "age-sets" of Maasai
kids who will stay together through all the stages of life. In fact,
the event we are attending is a coming-of-age ceremony, a ritual
for one age-set graduating to the next stage. Pilot will have his turn
in a few years, when his age-set goes from being boys to **MORANI**.

The Morani

The morani are the warriors of the Maasai. I think they're kinda cool and kinda scary at the same time. When the boys in a certain age-set all get to 13-16 years old, they go through initiation rites together to become warriors. In the old days, the morani protected the herds from raids by other clans or tribes, and especially from lions. Killing a lion was always the real test of courage. I'm glad they're rethinking that one.

The morani seem to have it made. They live in their own manyatta and have no trouble getting girls. They only eat meat and drink blood- for fierceness. They also spend a lot of time on their looks. Their hair is never cut. They braid it and then cake on this gunky red clay stuff. And they cover themselves with bracelets, necklaces, and all kinds of doodads. But I wouldn't mess with them - they never go anywhere without their swords.

When the age-set all reaches about 25-26 years old they go through another ritual together. Their moms shave off all those greasy long braids from their heads, marking the end of their time as morani. Now they become "junior elders", and can marry and start their own families.

Pilot's older brother, Lonkoi, is a morani. Mutongai wanted me to meet him, but he did NOT want to meet me. He even gave his dad a hard time for bringing me there. Mutongai just smiled and said "Don't take it personally - he's going through a phase. But be careful taking pictures. He could get ornery."

MORANI

the laibon
his wife his grandson

the PARTY GUESTS

MAASAI GIRLS

the joint was JUMPIN'

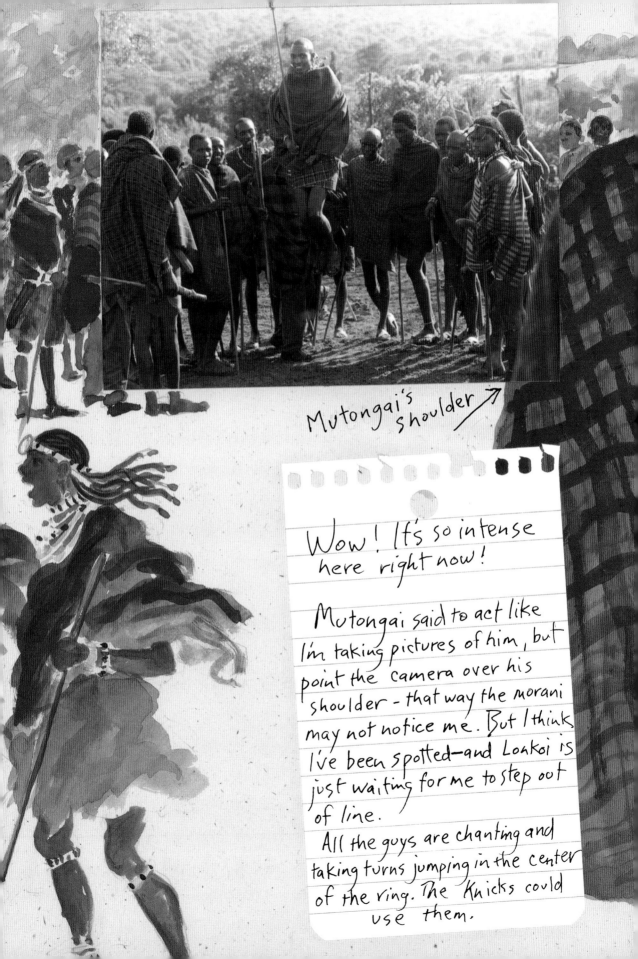

Mutongai's shoulder →

Wow! It's so intense here right now!

Mutongai said to act like I'm taking pictures of him, but point the camera over his shoulder - that way the morani may not notice me. But I think I've been spotted—and Lonkoi is just waiting for me to step out of line.

All the guys are chanting and taking turns jumping in the center of the ring. The Knicks could use them.

Here's the DOWNSIDE of living near wildlife, especially if you're a cow?

We were up all night because of all the racket coming from the animals outside the manyatta.

I was making Pilot laugh by "freaking" every time I heard a lion roar. But he stopped laughing when he heard the baboons call their "9-1-1."

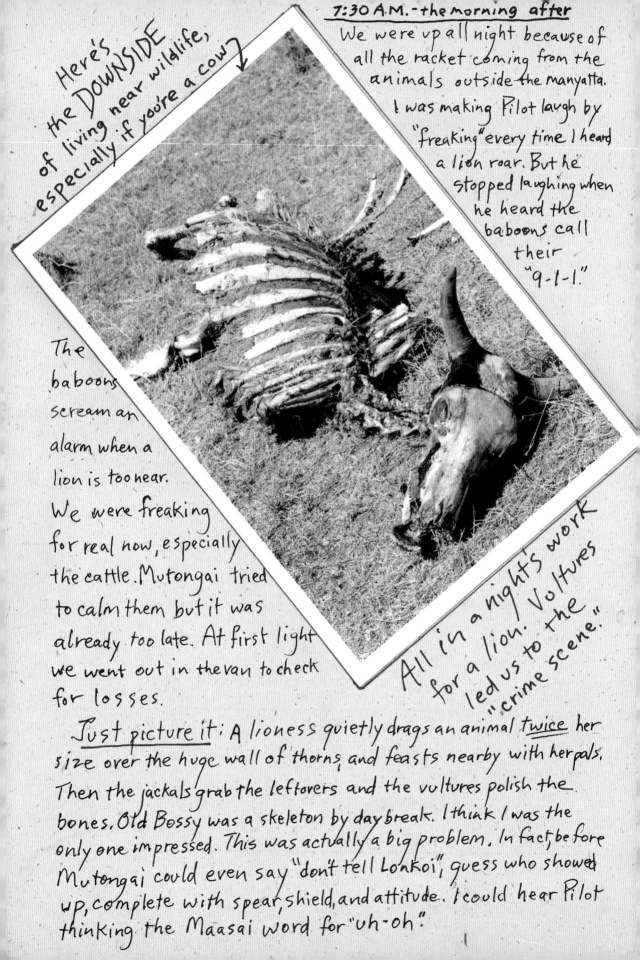

The baboons scream an alarm when a lion is too near. We were freaking for real now, especially the cattle. Mutongai tried to calm them but it was already too late. At first light we went out in the van to check for losses.

All in a night's work for a lion. Vultures led us to the "crime scene."

Just picture it: A lioness quietly drags an animal twice her size over the huge wall of thorns, and feasts nearby with her pals. Then the jackals grab the leftovers and the vultures polish the bones. Old Bossy was a skeleton by daybreak. I think I was the only one impressed. This was actually a big problem. In fact, before Mutongai could even say "don't tell Lonkoi", guess who showed up, complete with spear, shield, and attitude. I could hear Pilot thinking the Maasai word for "uh-oh".

It seems that a showdown between Mutongai and Lonkoi had been coming for some time. It came. Pilot and I ducked into the van, to avoid the cross fire. He explained what the yelling was about, but it was pretty obvious. Lonkoi was determined to get the lion and his dad was determined to stop him. I felt bad for Mutongai. After all, he was a morani once himself - maybe even killed a lion. Now he was trying to talk his son out of it. Didn't work.

Lonkoi and his morani buddies stormed away, over the savanna.

We were tense and silent all the way back to the manyatta.

morani status symbol #1

lion's mane hat
souvenir of a lion hunt.
Some old relative got
this one a long time ago, but
I guess Lonkoi wants
one of his own.

I asked Mutongai if the Maasai ever tried better fencing for their livestock. He showed me this new goat corral. The walls are

made of flattened oil drums, about 12 ft. high. The idea is that the big cats - even leopards - won't get any traction when they try to go up the metal sides. No place to dig in the claws.

But now something else is bugging Mutongai. He noticed that the wildebeest were coming into the area, gathering early for their big migration. Pilot's younger brother and sister are out there somewhere with the goats (they left this morning when we were away). The goat kids and human kids are pretty small. They could get in the way of a rowdy bunch of wildebeest. Pilot and I are gonna go look for them.

WHO LET THE GOATS OUT?

9:15 A.M.   WILDEBEEST MIGRATION

Whoa! Where did they come from? Yesterday there was just a handful here. All of a sudden, they got friends! Lots of 'em. How weird-one day they're standing and yawning, and the next they're running like their butts are on fire. Pilot said it's an early warm-up for the big migration. Twice a year (more or less), over 2 million animals gather into gigantic herds and head out in search of grass, traveling up and down a humongus plain called the Serengeti, in Tanzania, and the Maasai Mara in Kenya. Pilot said these local herds are getting pumped up to join in the ongoing "Mara-go-round" when it passes nearby.

Sept.

July

Maasai-Mara

Serengeti

Oct.

April   Nov.

Migration 🌓 Stats:
wildebeest: 1,400,000 (or more)
gazelles, impalas: 600,000
zebras: 200,000
length of total trip: 800 miles (+ or -)
(like New York to Chicago)

KENYA
TANZANIA

I've got a minute to write while Pilot uses my binoculars to look for signs of the kids with the kids. He just spotted them under a big tree - in a sea of wildebeest! Now what do we do? I hope they don't bite.

<u>12:15 P.M.</u> - What a trip! The 'beesties were like big, hairy schools of fish, swerving away from us as we shouted and clapped our way through them (I just followed Pilot's lead). But by the time we reached the kids, they had closed in around us again. More and more - everywhere - thousands of horns and hooves swirling around us. Just as I was about to ask, "What now?" a little white dot popped on to the horizon. It was Mutongai in the van! The 'beesties parted like the Red Sea as he drove toward our tree. We heaved the goats into the back of the van and took off. It was a riot to see the goats standing on Aunt Elaine's stuff. She'll never know. Anyway, I'm just glad we're out of that little spot.

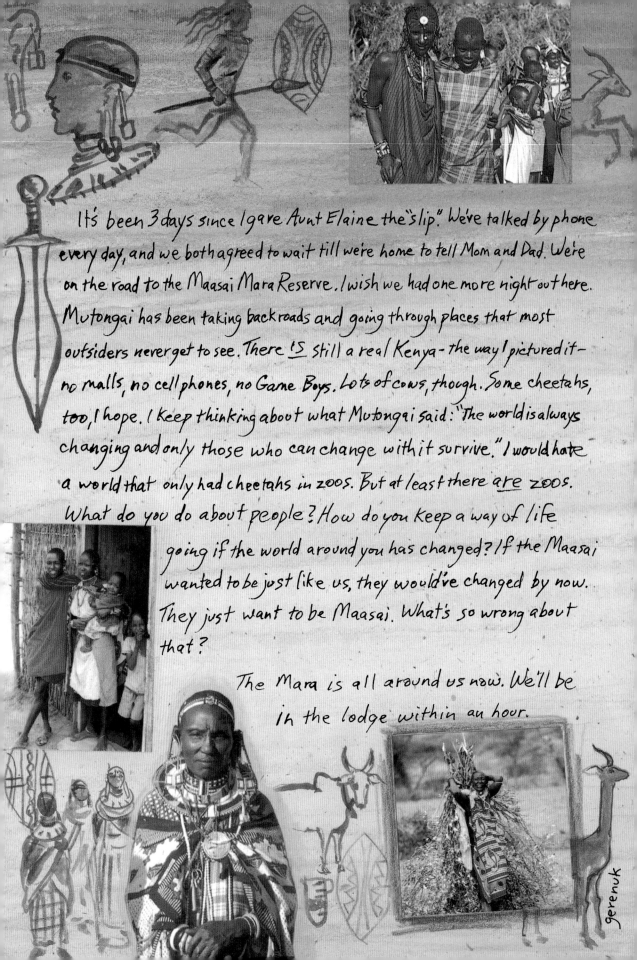

It's been 3 days since I gave Aunt Elaine the "slip." We've talked by phone every day, and we both agreed to wait till we're home to tell Mom and Dad. We're on the road to the Maasai Mara Reserve. I wish we had one more night out here. Mutongai has been taking back roads and going through places that most outsiders never get to see. There _IS_ still a real Kenya - the way I pictured it — no malls, no cell phones, no Game Boys. Lots of cows, though. Some cheetahs, too, I hope. I keep thinking about what Mutongai said: "The world is always changing and only those who can change with it survive." I would hate a world that only had cheetahs in zoos. But at least there _are_ zoos. What do you do about people? How do you keep a way of life going if the world around you has changed? If the Maasai wanted to be just like us, they would've changed by now. They just want to be Maasai. What's so wrong about that?

The Mara is all around us now. We'll be in the lodge within an hour.

gerenuk

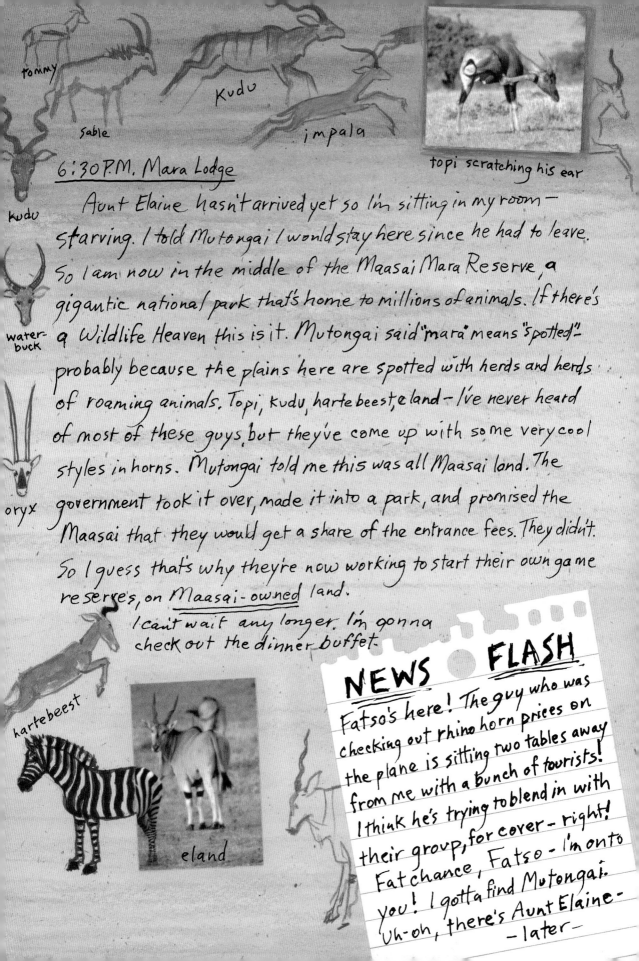

tommy

Kudu

sable

impala

topi scratching his ear

kudu

water-
buck

oryx

6:30 P.M. Mara Lodge

Aunt Elaine hasn't arrived yet so I'm sitting in my room — starving. I told Mutongai I would stay here since he had to leave. So I am now in the middle of the Maasai Mara Reserve, a gigantic national park that's home to millions of animals. If there's a Wildlife Heaven this is it. Mutongai said "mara" means "spotted" — probably because the plains here are spotted with herds and herds of roaming animals. Topi, kudu, hartebeest, eland — I've never heard of most of these guys, but they've come up with some very cool styles in horns. Mutongai told me this was all Maasai land. The government took it over, made it into a park, and promised the Maasai that they would get a share of the entrance fees. They didn't. So I guess that's why they're now working to start their own game reserves, on Maasai-owned land.

I can't wait any longer. I'm gonna check out the dinner buffet.

hartebeest

eland

NEWS FLASH

Fatso's here! The guy who was checking out rhino horn prices on the plane is sitting two tables away from me with a bunch of tourists! I think he's trying to blend in with their group, for cover — right! Fat chance, Fatso — I'm onto you! I gotta find Mutongai. Uh-oh, there's Aunt Elaine —
— later —

<u>1:30 P.M. Mara Lodge</u>

I spoke to Mutongai this morning before he left for the day with Aunt Elaine. He said for me to keep an eye on Fatso until he could find out more about him. There may be nothing to find out. But I don't like the smell of him (in so many ways). For one thing, his "tourist" act is totally lame. What tourist gets phone calls out in the middle of Africa? He's on the phone right now. I can watch him from my window — he's by the pool. Actually, he's coming this way, looking for a place where he can't be overheard, no doubt. Hey — wait a second...

I <u>just got a major break</u>! Fatso brought the phone next to my window — I could hear everything! I dove between the beds so he couldn't see me, grabbed the pad off the phone table, and started scribbling notes. He was speaking a real mish-mosh of English and Swahili (Swahinglish?) He even used that dopey "useful phrase" sheet they passed out on the plane (glad I still have mine). The one word I understood right away was **KIFARU** — "rhino" — something is <u>definitely</u> going down with rhinos somewhere. I gotta find Pilot but I don't want Fatso to see me leave.

This was weird — he repeated these words slow and loud — like it was the most important thing he had to say.

Mara Lodge
Safari Clubs of Kenya , Ltd.
^^^^^^^^^^^^^^^^^^^^^^^^^^^^^

Oscar
Lucy
Charley
Hotel
Oscar
Romeo
Oscar

Useful Swahili Phrases

Hello	Jambo (Jambo sana)
How are you?	Habari?
Well	Mzuri
Thanks	Ahsante (sana)
Please	Tafadhali
Bring me	Lete
I would like	Ningependa
Quickly	Upesi
Today	Leo
Tomorrow	Kesho
Food	Chakula
Water	Maji
Medicine	Dawa
Coffee	Kahawa
Beer	Pombe
Tea	Chai
Milk	Maziwa
Meat	Nyama
Fish	Samaki
Butter	Siagi
Sugar	Sukari
Hot	Moto
Cold	Baridi
Many	Nyingi
Welcome	Karibu
Yes	Ndio
No	Hapana
How much?	Ngapi?
I would like a	Ningependa
cold beer	pombe baridi
One/Two/Three	Moja/Mbili/Tatu
Four/Five/Six	Nne/Tano/Sita
Seven/Eight	Saba/Nane
Nine/Ten	Tisa/Kumi
Eleven etc.	Kumi na moja etc.
Twenty	Ishirini
Twenty-one etc.	Ishirini na moja etc.
Thirty/Forty	Thelathini/Arubaini
Fifty/Sixty	Hamsini/Sitini
Seventy/Eighty	Sabini/Themanini
Ninety/Hundred	Tisini/Mia moja
Two hundred etc.	Mia mbili etc.
Thousand	Elfu
Where is?	Wapi?
— the toilet	Choo
— a telephone	Simu
— a petrol station	Kituo cha Petroli
— a mechanic	Fundi
— the nearest doctor	Daktari wa karibu
— a chemist's shop	Duka la Dawa
Left	Kushoto
Right	Kulia
Good-bye	Kwaheri

Mara Lodge
Safari Clubs of Kenya ,Ltd.

Kifaru

ngapi

elfu leo
elfu Kesho
Kisho?

wapi wapi
Kishoto A-tong
Kulia Kilariti

ndio leo nane

today eight - that means
tonight - something's happening
tonight at 8 - but what?
Pilot's over in the workers'
village babysitting his
cousin while his aunt goes
to town - hope I can find
him.

We learned the Navy Code
in scouts - it uses the 1st letter
of words to spell out another word
I think that's it
    O L C H O R O
So what's an olchoro"?
- couldn't find it on the animal list - in Swahili or English

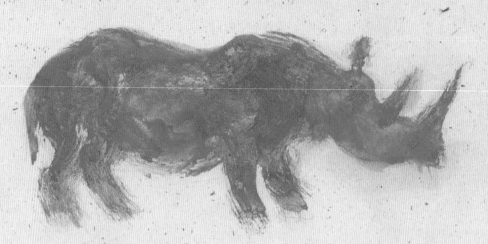

Oh my gosh - we figured it out! I think. When I found Pilot and showed him the notes it took him a minute - but then it hit him! Ol Choro isn't an animal - it's a place. <u>Ol Choro-Oiroua</u> - it's the wildlife sanctuary that Mutongai was talking about - the Maasai own it and have two rhinos there now. Those are the two that Fatso's targeting! He's got a deal going with somebody to get a horn - or two. Here's how we pieced it together:

<u>elfu leo elfu kesho</u> = 1000 today, 1000 tomorrow - probably dollars - Pilot said his dad told him poachers always want to be paid in $, getting half up front, before they go hunting, and half when they deliver the thing - which means they probably still haven't killed a rhino - yet.

<u>Kushoto Aitong Kulia Kiloriti</u> = left at Aitong right at Kiloriti directions to the meeting place - it's on the way to Ol Choro.

Pilot's out looking for a neighbor to dump his cousin on so we can get going, so I'm watching her (actually, she's watching me) till he gets back. I'm not sure what we're gonna do, but it's gotta happen now.

I just wish Mutongai would show up.

Midnight

Everything happened so fast once we jumped on the back of that truck. Pilot knew of one leaving the lodge that would be going by Kiloriti. We still didn't have a real plan, but we knew Fatso had to be on this road—it's the only one. By the time we jumped out night was falling, and the hyenas were already calling to each other. We grabbed a couple of big sticks. As if they weren't enough, a line of black shapes appeared on the horizon. Elephants—a big herd, probably less than a ½ mile from us. They generally avoid humans, but they <u>hate</u> to be surprised—that's when they charge. I prayed the wind wouldn't give our scent away. One good thing about the savanna—you can see everything from a long way off. A lone pair of headlights was winding along the road we had just traveled. Fatso—on his evil way to his evil meeting. He slowed down and blinked his lights when he reached the turn. Another pair of lights blinked back from a grove of acacias. The fat man slowly drove off the road toward the trees. Darkness was on our side now. We followed like shadows crossing the ground and found cover near the poachers' camp. A tree with some low branches made a good lookout. The poachers made a fire to keep away the elephants. It lit up the ivory tusks leaning against their car. It looked like they were trying to get an extra sale out of their customer.

Suddenly Pilot jumped. We looked down and saw a hand gripping his ankle. Lonkoi! It seemed as if he had appeared from nowhere. At that moment I didn't care how he got there - I was just glad to see him.

A moment later another set of headlights appeared on the road behind us. The poachers put out the fire and picked up their guns. Only their enemies would be out here after dark- patrols of the Kenya Wildlife Service. But I knew the sound of that car.

"Mutongai," Pilot whispered.

The four poachers lifted their guns and aimed. Fatso slipped back into his car.

The wind shifted. The elephants had moved close enough to see that many had their trunks raised in the air, sniffing danger. Lonkoi studied their moves from his hiding place in the bushes. From our vantage point we could see that the queen elephant was now at the edge of the grove, dangerously close to the poachers. But they stayed glued in the opposite direction, toward the oncoming van.

A calf wandered out into the open, behind the gunmen, but when the queen came to steer the baby back to the herd Lonkoi saw his moment. He rushed out toward the calf, screaming like a maniac! Then he veered away and darted into the grove on the far side of the camp. The poachers spun around and fired into the dark. The old queen flapped her ears and charged, with the herd behind her. The poachers fired again but then dropped their guns and ran for their lives. The hunters became the hunted as the queen chased them through the trees and onto the plains. Fatso peeled out in the other direction. Mutongai took off after him. The elephants were focused on smashing up the poachers' Jeep, giving us a chance to escape. Lonkoi popped out of the bushes unharmed and signaled to run with the wind. I didn't know I could run so fast. In my head nothing mattered but the wind direction and that look of elephant rage.

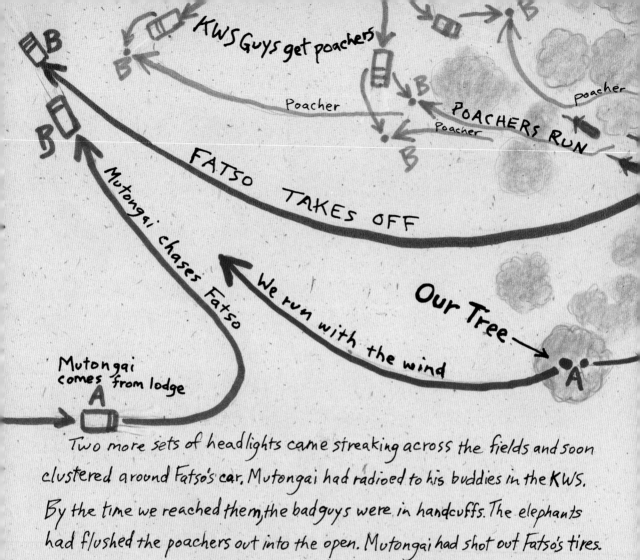

KWS Guys get poachers

Poacher

Poacher

POACHERS RUN

Poacher

Poacher

FATSO TAKES OFF

Mutongai chases Fatso

We run with the wind

Our Tree

Mutongai comes from lodge

A

A

Two more sets of headlights came streaking across the fields and soon clustered around Fatso's car. Mutongai had radioed to his buddies in the KWS. By the time we reached them, the bad guys were in handcuffs. The elephants had flushed the poachers out into the open. Mutongai had shot out Fatso's tires. Within an hour the elephants were gone and the bad guys were on their way to be booked. We went back to the poachers' camp to collect the tusks.

Then came the surprise. As we drove up to the overturned Jeep, a fuzzy little round shape stumbled into our headlights. A baby elephant had been left behind. Mutongai said it had to be an orphan. An elephant mom would never leave her baby. The calf's mother was probably killed by these very poachers. The baby would be a lion's meal by dawn if we left her here. Mutongai said there was only one place for her – the baby elephant orphanage in Nairobi. We got to ride with her to the KWS station. That's where I am right now, waiting for Mutongai to finish writing the report on tonight's events. The Kenya Wildlife Service (KWS) is the Law around here.

It's near midnight now and even though I'm wiped out I wanted to

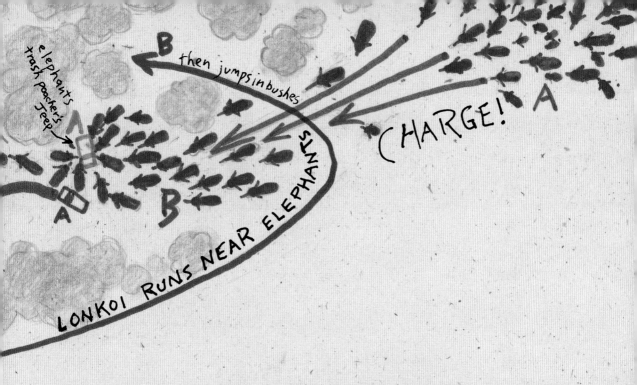

write all this stuff down while its still fresh. I told Mutongai that it was
so cool how he could use his hunting instincts to find us. He said actually
his niece told him, the one who Pilot was babysitting for. She followed the
whole thing when Pilot and I were figuring out the code. Pretty impressive!
But the one Mutongai is proudest of is Lonkoi. And with good reason.
Lonkoi had tracked down that cow-stealing lion, but then decided to
let it live. He left his friends and wandered alone for many days, thinking about it. That's when he saw the poachers' fire and discovered
us. I don't really know what all that means to him but I guess there's
one more lion alive tonight because of it.

    Now the only thing left to do is explain   all this to Aunt Elaine.
Mutongai has already radioed back to the lodge to let her know
that I'm ok. It's funny - it all seemed to happen so fast, but now
when I think about the lodge it feels like a lifetime ago
when we left it.

Noon – Nairobi

I knew this day was gonna come sooner than I wanted it to. I'll be glad to see Mom and Dad and even that warthog piglet Sally, but I'm not ready to go yet. Our flight back is at 10 P.M. tonight, but I feel like I've got more stuff to do here. I want to see where it all goes now - how it works out with the rhinos, and with Loukoi, starting work with the KWS, and Mutongai helping to develop the Maasai wildlife reserves. At least I can keep up with Pilot until I come back. Aunt Elaine gave his school her laptop so he and I can e-mail each other.

So much has happened since that night when the poachers were caught. The next day the newspapers covered it. Even the people at the lodge made a big deal out of us. The coolest part was getting to meet Chief Ole Ntutu, the Paramount Chief of the Kenya Maasai. He wanted to thank us, so we drove up to his house at Ol Choro Oiroua, where the two rhinos live. It was great to see them alive and well and safe. I liked what the chief said. "This land would not be Kenya without our wild animal neighbors living here too," he said. "Protecting the rhinos is not just for the good of the animals, or for the Maasai, but for all Kenyans."

Even Aunt Elaine got into it! She donated her fee from the fashion shoot to the Ol Choro Oiroua Wildlife Association. She still hasn't gotten the hang of discipline - fortunately. It didn't take much to talk her into letting me ride back to Nairobi in the truck with Mutongai, Pilot, and the baby elephant. Good ol' wacky Aunt Elaine. I knew she would come through.

The elephant orphanage folks were happy to take in a new baby. Their first elephant orphan came to them over twenty years ago and they've been rescuing and caring for them ever since. The most important thing for a baby is family, and that's what ours will get there. Still, it was hard to say goodbye to her on the same day I had to say goodbye to Mutongai and Pilot. The orphanage let Pilot and me name her. We decided to call her Mara. I thought that was the perfect name. It makes it easier to leave tonight. Now I know I'll be back, to be part of what happens to Mara.

For more information, please contact the Loita Maasai Foundation,
P.O. Box 25021, Nairobi, Kenya (www.Loita-Maasai.com, e-mail: grootenh@iconnect.co.ke);
Friends of Conservation, 1520 Kensington Road, Suite 201, Oak Brook, IL 60521; The David Sheldrick
Wildlife Trust (www.sheldrickwildlifetrust.org); or World Wildlife Fund (www.worldwildlifefund.org).

This book is dedicated to Jackson OleKasha, Emmanuel Onetu, Paramount Chief Ole Ntutu,
and all those who share a vision of hope for the future of the Maasai.

Special thanks to Christopher Norbury; Frederique Grootenhuis; Neil Thomas;
Paula Wiseman; Amanda Hudson; the Sonkoi family; and most of all to
Dr. Jan Geu Grootenhuis,
whose vision, knowledge, and passion for a sustainable world has inspired this book.

www.hudsontalbott.com

Safari Journal is a work of fiction based on the author's research and travels through Africa. Although some of the
experiences described in the book are drawn from real life, the characters are all creations of the author's imagination.

Library of Congress Cataloging-in-Publication Data
Talbott, Hudson.
Safari journal/by Hudson Talbott.
p. cm.
"Silver Whistle."
Summary: Twelve-year-old Carey is unhappy about being sent on a trip to Kenya with his wacky Aunt Elaine,
until he encounters fascinating customs, endangered animals, and wild adventures.
[1. Kenya—Fiction. 2. Poaching—Fiction. 3. Endangered species—Fiction. 4. Jungle animals—Fiction.
5. Aunts—Fiction. 6. Adventure and adventurers—Fiction.] I. Title.
PZ7.T153Saf 2003
[Fic]—dc21   2002006372
ISBN 0-15-216393-X

First edition
A C E G H F D B

The illustrations in this book were done in watercolor, colored pencil, pen and ink, and felt-tipped pens,
with photographs by the author, on textured paper embedded with seed husks.
The display type and text type were hand-lettered by Hudson Talbott.
Color separations by Bright Arts Ltd., Hong Kong
Printed and bound by Tien Wah Press, Singapore
This book was printed on totally chlorine-free Enso Stora Matte paper.
Production supervision by Sandra Grebenar and Pascha Gerlinger
Conceptual design by Hudson Talbott
Graphic design by Linda Lockowitz